Reader Books Weekly Reader Books

1983

Ashleigh

miller

Weekly Reader Books presents

mystery of the forgotten island

Florence Parry Heide and Roxanne Heide

Text illustrations by Seymour Fleishman

ALBERT WHITMAN & COMPANY, Chicago

This book is a presentation of
Weekly Reader Books.

Weekly Reader Books offers
book clubs for children from
preschool through junior high school.
All quality hardcover books are selected by
a distinguished Weekly Reader Selection Board.

For further information write to:
Weekly Reader Books
1250 Fairwood Ave.
Columbus, Ohio 43216

Library of Congress Cataloging in Publication Data

Heide, Florence Parry.
    Mystery of the forgotten island.

    (Pilot books)
    SUMMARY: The Spotlight Club detectives
discover strange happenings and stage a thrilling
rescue on a forgotten island in the north woods.
    [1. Mystery and detective stories] I. Heide,
Roxanne, joint author.   II. Fleishman, Seymour.
III. Title.
PZ7.H36Myeh   [Fic]   79-18367
ISBN 0-8075-5376-X

Cover illustration by E.F. Habbas

Contents

1 • *Mysterious Island*

CINDY TEMPLE plunged backwards into the cool, inviting water, giving a little scream before she went under. In another minute her brother Jay and their best friend Dexter Tate had followed her into the lake.

"Wow!" sputtered Cindy as she came up for air. "Terrific!"

The two boys surfaced, splashing water around them.

"I told you it would be cold!" called a voice from the pier. Mary Beech, a girl Cindy's age, sat cross-legged at the end, smiling at the three Spotlighters.

"And you were right, Mary B.," Cindy agreed. "Cold. But beautiful."

She wiped wet strands of hair from her forehead and swam closer to the pier. "What would we have done this summer if you and your dad hadn't invited us up here to your cottage?"

Mary B. laughed. "Knowing you three, you'd have thought of something. You probably would have found another mystery to solve."

"Hey, Mary B., jump in and join us!" shouted Dexter from the water.

Mary B. shook her head and frowned, then pointed to her side.

Cindy looked at her friend with concern and climbed back onto the pier. "What's the matter?"

"A dumb old sideache," said Mary B. "It was bothering me all night, off and on. Must have been all those roasted marshmallows we ate last night around the campfire."

"It was probably the ghost stories we told," Cindy said.

Just then an engine roared, and they all glanced toward the boathouse. Two men were standing inside, studying a motor. Mary B. put her hands over her ears and made a face. "I'll be glad when Dad gets the engine to his boat fixed. He's been hovering over that thing with Guy ever since we got up here yesterday."

"Well, if anyone can fix an engine, it's Guy Sanderson, right?" Dexter said, smiling over at the ruddy-faced man they had met earlier in the morning.

"You bet," Mary B. said. "He can fix anything—from water pumps to gas leaks to engines. Lucky for the summer people up here on the chain of lakes there's someone like Guy around. He's here all year, so he can check on the cottages during the winter. And he's the best fishing guide that was ever born."

There was a big splash behind Cindy. Jay and Dexter were leapfrogging their way to the pier.

"Why don't you three take the rowboat out before supper?" asked Mary B., nodding toward the boat that was tied to the other side of the pier. "There's lots of time."

"That sounds like a good idea," Cindy said, looking at the boys. "It would be fun to explore the chain of lakes. This lake goes into the next one, right?"

"Right," said Mary B. "Most of the lakes around here are connected."

"Why don't you come with us, Mary B.?" asked Jay.

Mary B. shook her head. "I've got some things to check out. This is our first weekend here this summer, and I want to get my fishing gear squared away for tomorrow. Besides—" She put her hand to her side again.

Another flicker of worry crossed Cindy's face. "Sure you're okay?" she asked.

Mary B. laughed. "Dad's here to take care of me in case I get sick. But if anyone's going to need help, it's you guys, trying to maneuver that clunky old rowboat."

Jay climbed out of the water and picked up a beach towel to throw over his shoulders. "At camp last year we learned how to handle a stubborn rowboat, didn't we, Dex?"

Dexter followed Jay out of the water and took his glasses from the edge of the pier. "You're right," he said, smiling. "We could handle any kind of boat after that."

"Well, what are we waiting for?" asked Jay.

"Let's get out of our wet suits and take the rowboat for a spin."

The three chased each other up the hill to the cottage. In a few minutes they were dry, dressed, and seated in the rowboat.

"You'll need life preservers," Mary B. shouted to the Spotlighters. "They're in the boathouse. I'll get them."

She walked into the boathouse, her hand still on her side.

Dexter sat in the middle of the rowboat. "I'll row first, okay?" he asked.

"I'll be navigator," said Jay.

"And I'll be the passenger," said Cindy. "After a while we can switch jobs."

Jay untied the boat, and they shoved off.

"First stop, boathouse," said Dexter, clumsily trying to turn the boat around. "It will just take me a couple of minutes to get back into the swing of rowing," he assured Jay and Cindy, looking over his shoulder and heading around the pier toward the boathouse.

By the time Dexter had managed to bring the rowboat to the big open door of the boathouse,

Mary B. was coming out with the life preservers over her arm.

"How's the pain in your side, honey?" asked Mr. Beech with a concerned smile. He was a tall, slender man with a face like Mary B.'s—long with high cheekbones and dimples.

"I told it to go away. That should do the trick."

Mr. Beech put his arm around his daughter and issued instructions to Cindy, Jay, and Dexter. "Here—three life preservers for three kids. One for each passenger—it's the law." He tossed the orange jackets into the boat. "Tomorrow we'll go fishing in the big motorboat," he added. "Guy will have the motor fixed by then for sure."

"I'll be taking you to the very best fishing spots," Guy said. He rubbed the reddish stubble on his chin. "I promise by this time tomorrow you'll be frying fish for supper."

"Perfect!" said Dexter, reaching for the oars.

Guy put up a hand. "Just a sec, kids." He took out a folded paper from the pocket of his red plaid shirt. "This is a map I made of the lakes around here. It will help you figure out where you're going."

"And how to get back," added Mr. Beech.

"Usually I charge a dollar for this map, but since you're friends of the Beeches, we'll consider it a gift."

"Be sure to hang onto that map," Mr. Beech advised. "All the best fishing places are marked on it."

Jay took the map. "Since I'm navigator, I'll be in charge. Thanks a million, Guy."

"This chain of lakes is like a maze," Guy said. "Be sure to leave yourselves plenty of time to get back before sundown. Head east and north. If you go south, you'll get into marshes and swampland."

Jay glanced at the map and nodded.

"Don't go too far," Guy added.

Dexter rowed the boat away from the pier. Mary, Guy, and Mr. Beech all waved.

"Good luck!" Mary B. shouted.

In a few minutes Dexter, Jay, and Cindy were out of sight of the boathouse. Cindy sat at the back of the boat, gazing contentedly at the shoreline. Jay perched at the bow and studied Guy's map.

There were a lot of lakes—some big, some small. All were joined, though sometimes only by narrow passages. Intricate lines on the map showed which areas of water were deep and which were shallow. A large shaded part was labeled "Swamp." Guy had numbered the best fishing spots, and on the back of the map he had written the best times of day to fish in different places.

Cindy looked at the tall pine trees hugging the shore. From the boat you couldn't tell whether there were any cottages behind the trees. Maybe there weren't. Mr. Beech had told them last night that there were very few summer homes nearby. He'd also said that most of the people who owned cottages waited until July to come. Now it was only the middle of June. "The closest neighbor we've got right now is Guy," he'd told them, "and even Guy lives a couple of lakes away."

Cindy shifted position and sighed happily. Lazy thoughts drifted through her mind. "Want me to row?" she asked Dexter after a while.

He shook his head. "You can row on the way back. I'm just getting the rhythm."

Jay had been studying the map, and now he was frowning. He could see that they had entered a small lake that seemed to have no outlet.

Cindy leaned over and trailed her hand in the water. "Where are we?" she asked Jay.

Jay turned the map upside down. "I think I've been reading the map backwards," he confessed. "I thought we were going the other direction. This is a dead end. I see where we are on the map, but Guy's marked this as swamp."

"Some navigator," Dexter told Jay. He wiped his forehead with his arm and looked around.

Cindy leaned forward. "Look over there. I just saw an opening in the reeds. Maybe it's another channel."

"I'll row closer," said Dexter. As they drew near the spot, they saw that the softly swaying reeds concealed a narrow channel. Dexter headed into it. The passageway twisted and turned for a time, so they couldn't see what was ahead. Then the channel widened. Ahead of them lay a small lake—and an island.

"An island!" said Jay.

Dexter headed toward it.

Tall reeds whispered against the boat as they came close to land. Then a small sandy beach appeared, hemmed in by towering pine trees. The Spotlighters quickly climbed out and pulled the rowboat up on shore.

"Nice," Jay said softly, looking around. There was no sound. The sand was smooth and untouched except for tiny animal trackings. The scent of pine was strong and sweet. Jay and Cindy secured the rowboat, tying the anchor rope around a tree.

"Beautiful," Cindy whispered. "A paradise. An island paradise not on the map."

"The forgotten island," Dexter added.

"Let's check it out," Jay suggested.

"Right," Dexter said. "Let's explore."

"This is so peaceful," Cindy said, sitting down on the sand. "I'm just going to sit here and pretend I'm stranded on a lovely paradise island all by myself." She sifted sand through her fingers and stared out at the reeds and the sparkling blue water. Then she lay back and looked at the blue sky and the white clouds.

"Suit yourself," Jay told her. "But you may miss something exciting."

"Like running into a bear?" asked Cindy, raising her eyebrows. "Well, I'll stay and guard the boat in case we have to make a quick getaway."

"Let's all meet back here in half an hour," Dexter suggested, looking at his watch.

Cindy waved as the boys headed into the woods. In a few minutes she could no longer hear the crackling of their feet on the thick carpet of pine needles.

She searched around for small flat rocks to skip. When she had a handful, she slowly skimmed one after another into the water beyond the reeds. Then she watched a big, low-flying bird screech and swoop and take off again, soaring into the sunlight.

Pretty soon she sat down and leaned against a tall pine. She gazed lazily up at the tops of the trees.

Suddenly she stiffened. There was somebody near her. She could feel it. Slowly, Cindy looked around. She saw no one, and yet she knew someone was very close to her, watching.

The silence was broken by the sound of twigs crackling behind her. Still sitting, she spun around, searching for a movement. A shadow glided behind a tree. Something or someone was there, within yards of her. Was it an animal?

"Who's there?" Cindy asked.

There was no answer, only the silence of the woods. Cindy was uneasy. She had felt something there, something threatening. She stood up. Was it her imagination? After all, she wasn't used to the different forest sounds. Maybe she had only heard a squirrel or a bird. Still—

Keeping her eyes on the thick cluster of trees in front of her, she walked slowly backwards to the boat.

There. There it was again. Now she saw a

shadow moving between the trees. Someone was watching her. Someone wearing a big hat. Someone who didn't want to be seen.

2 • The Prisoner

WHEN THE BOYS left Cindy on the beach, they walked single file, picking their way through the undergrowth and the towering evergreens. Pine needles scrunched under their feet.

"Maybe we're the first human beings to walk on this island," said Dexter. "Maybe we've discovered new land."

They had gone only a short way when Jay stopped suddenly. Dexter nearly ran into him.

The boys stared. Beyond the trees was a grassy clearing. And standing in the clearing was a big old house. A long screened porch ran along one side of it.

"Someone lives here," said Dexter, disappointed. "And I was just beginning to feel like a real explorer."

"The owners don't like trespassers," said Jay, pointing to a high chain-link fence. It looked new.

"Why would anyone want to put up a fence like that here in the wilderness?" asked Dexter. "To keep someone or something out—or to keep someone or something in?"

Dexter and Jay moved closer to the fence and the house. There was no sign of activity.

"Let's see what the back of the house looks like," suggested Jay. Dexter nodded. There were trees along the fence that hid the boys as they went around to the back.

"Why do I feel like a sneak?" Jay asked. He crouched lower and lower.

"Because you're sneaking," Dexter whispered.

They reached the back of the house. White-painted furniture was spread across a neatly trimmed lawn. At the far end of the yard a small grove of pine trees grew inside the fence.

As they approached the grove of pine trees, the boys felt suddenly awkward.

"Maybe we shouldn't be here," Jay said. What if someone was watching them? They stared through the fence and the trees at the lawn.

"Is there someone there?" came a quiet voice.

Dexter and Jay froze.

"I heard you," someone said. "I haven't lost my hearing yet. Speak up, friends."

The boys edged closer to the sound of the voice. Finally Jay cleared his throat. "It's just us," he said. "Dexter Tate and me, Jay Temple. We didn't mean to trespass or anything, but we saw this island and decided to—"

"I don't need your excuses," came the voice. "I'm glad you've come."

Dexter and Jay exchanged glances. They heard a squeak, as if someone were rising from a chair. Suddenly they faced an old man, his gnarled hands tightly gripping a black cane. Neatly trimmed white hair capped the man's head. He wore a tan sport shirt.

"Please don't hesitate," he said with a smile. "I want very much to make your acquaintance." He stretched a hand toward the fence, then shook his head. "I'm afraid the fence prevents me from introducing myself properly. Please, if you will, follow me to the gate and we shall appropriately introduce ourselves. But be very quiet. We don't want them to know you're here."

Who was "them"? Jay wondered

The old man walked off slowly, motioning to the boys and leaning heavily on his cane. Jay and Dexter followed on the other side of the fence. In a few moments they came to a gate that was held shut by a heavy padlock.

"It's not locked," said the old man. "They know I can't open it anyway, with my arthritis. But we must be careful. If you are seen, there will be trouble." He pointed in the direction of the house.

"The trees shield us, you see. They cannot see us. Always in the afternoons they play backgammon and talk secretly."

He leaned more heavily on his cane. "And now if you'll open the padlock," he suggested.

Dexter gave the padlock a hard twist and lifted it out of the latch. The boys stepped inside the yard.

"Follow me," the old man said. "Your coming is a miracle. Yes, this is a much needed, long delayed miracle."

The boys exchanged glances and then followed the man to a clearing in the pine grove where an ornate white table stood with several chairs around it. An empty pitcher was on the table, with a half-empty glass of lemonade next to it. Piles of books were spread on the table and chairs and even the ground. The man cleared off two chairs and then held his hand out to the boys. "I'm Alan Whitson," he said.

Jay introduced himself and Dexter. When Mr. Whitson sat down, the boys pulled their chairs close to hear his quiet voice. "This is a beautiful jail, as jails go," Mr. Whitson said. "And my jailors—Lorrie, my late son's daughter, and her rather overbearing husband, John—are very kind. Kind jailors, but nevertheless I am a prisoner here."

Jay and Dexter looked at one another. A prisoner? What did Mr. Whitson mean? The old man leaned forward earnestly, shaking his head.

"Lorrie brought me here three months ago with promises of carefree days. There was no fence when she brought me.

"The island has been my summer home for many years. I can't tell you how many hours I spent up here in the old days—fishing, hiking, camping, dreaming." He smiled wistfully. "Now it's the dreaming part I prefer. That's about all I can do anymore. All that I'm permitted to do, anyway."

He gestured toward a birchbark canoe just outside the chain-link fence. "When I first came, I fixed up the old canoe. For old times sake, before my arthritis got so bad. Even if I could manage it, they'd never let me take it out on the water. They don't trust me. The canoe and I are landlocked." Mr. Whitson sighed and leaned back, closing his eyes. "It's true. I'm a prisoner on my own island."

Jay and Dexter looked at each other uneasily. Was someone really holding the old man prisoner?

"Lorrie tells me I'm free to make my own decisions. But it's odd that she would install such a foreboding fence to insure me of freedom, isn't it? She and her husband claim that I might get lost without it. Lost? Lost on the island where I grew up, where I raised my children? Nonsense."

"Couldn't you leave if you wanted to?" asked Jay.

Mr. Whitson looked at him thoughtfully. "How?" he asked. "No, son, they won't let me go. They won't even let me walk down to the beach alone. They say I might fall. True, I'm a bit lame in my old age, but I still have a lot of energy left. It's not right, not right!" He thrust the tip of his cane forcefully into the ground.

Jay and Dexter were silent.

"I have a daughter, Cassie," Mr. Whitson continued. "She and I used to sit out here like this together. It didn't matter whether we talked or not. Just being together was important. We'd laugh and figure out the great mysteries of life."

If his daughter made him so happy, Jay wondered, why was Mr. Whitson so sad? Had something happened to her?

As if reading his mind, Mr. Whitson went on. "I'm quite worried about Cassie. Something's not right. She used to write me regularly, but since I've been a prisoner on this island, I've received only one letter from her. Only one letter in three months.

"Oh, nothing's been right since I came here," he went on. "Nothing. Things that started out as curious puzzles, like this fence, have turned into nightmarish problems. Nightmarish," he repeated.

He leaned forward earnestly. "There's evil festering here on this island—evil!"

3 • An Evil Spell

THE BOYS SHIVERED. Suddenly the air seemed chilly, in spite of the bright sun.

Was there really something evil about this beautiful place?

Before they could ask a question, Mr. Whitson said, "There's something odd, something wrong. The facts prove one thing, but my brain tells me the facts are misleading." He reached into the pocket of his shirt and withdrew a folded piece of paper.

"This is the letter Cassie sent me—the only letter she's written since I've been a prisoner on this island.

And Cassie is as close to me as my skin!" He blinked. "Closer, closer."

He unfolded the letter. The boys could see that it was typed. The paper was worn and smudged. Mr. Whitson must have read the letter dozens of times, Dexter thought.

"First you must understand that Cassie and I have always believed this island must stay as it is," the old man said. "It's always been a refuge—a quiet, safe place for people, animals, birds, and trees. For nature." He rubbed his hand over his eyes. "Knowing Cassie feels as I do, I made arrangements in my will for her to inherit this property. I knew she would keep it as it was meant to be kept."

He held the letter up to them. "But now she writes that she wants to sell the island, once it's hers, to a company that will turn it into a big resort of some kind. A resort—a gaudy, blaring tourist trap! That's what this letter says. And she signed it, all right. I'd know her signature anywhere. She always put a little heart over the *i* in her first name when she wrote me. It was a special bond between us."

His face was drawn and pale. "Something just isn't right." He shook his head slowly as he stared at the worn piece of paper on his lap. "I've written to her many times. She does not answer. And she does not come to the island. My dead son's daughter, Lorrie, tells me not to fret so over Cassie," he continued. "She says that it's obvious Cassie has lost interest in me and that she doesn't need me anymore. Lorrie says Cassie doesn't need my money, either. Cassie's got a business of her own and is doing well. Lorrie and her husband John, on the other hand, have made it very clear that *they* need the money."

He looked at the boys. "Lorrie and John want me to change my will in their favor. They promise to keep the island as it is now, a beautiful natural refuge. They tell me—and this letter tells me—that my Cassie will ruin it. Ruin it!"

He folded the letter and returned it to his pocket.

"Then you're going to change your will?" asked Jay.

"I have no choice," said Mr. Whitson, his voice cracking for the first time. "Why hasn't Cassie written? Why hasn't she come? Why is she so changed?" He held his head in his hands. "It's as if she's under a spell. An evil spell."

"Maybe you could telephone her," Dexter suggested. "Maybe you could talk to her and make her understand that the island should stay the way it is."

Mr. Whitson took a deep breath. "I sent word to her when I realized Lorrie was bringing me here. Cassie was in Europe at the time. Of course, she must be back in Los Angeles by now."

He tapped his pocket. "This is the only letter I've received, and I've written to her many times, asking her to reconsider. There is no telephone here on the island, or I would have tried to call her." He shook his head wearily.

"If only I could see her. If only I could be convinced that she really wants to sell this island. The letter—" He shook his head. "The letter doesn't sound as if it was written by my Cassie."

He pointed toward the house. "They don't want me to see her." He stared at Jay and Dexter. "They will do anything—*anything*—to keep her from me! They say it's for my own good, but I think they're lying."

He hesitated for a moment. "They're going to take me away from here tomorrow unless I sign everything over to them. This island and everything else I own." He seemed to shrink in his chair. "Then Cassie could never find me if she wanted to—never." He frowned. "So I'll sign the will they have prepared, leaving everything to them. If I don't sign, I have no doubt John and Lorrie will keep me from seeing Cassie again."

The boys were silent, their thoughts racing. Lorrie and John were going to make Mr. Whitson sign a will giving the island and everything else to them!

Mr. Whitson suddenly smiled. "I have an idea. Your coming here has solved a difficult problem. You can help me."

"How?" the boys asked at the same time.

"You must come back to this island tomorrow. That is very important. When you come, I will give you an envelope addressed to my lawyer. He is a lifelong friend. You will mail the envelope for me." He spread his hands. "See? It is simple." He waited, smiling, for them to say something, but they were silent.

"You see," he went on, "Lorrie and John would never mail it for me."

"What will the envelope have in it?" asked Dexter.

"A new will that I shall write by hand. In it I shall give this island to Cassie—but only if my lawyer is satisfied that she plans to keep the island for herself, and not sell it to promoters. I shall enclose a letter to him, explaining everything. You see? It is simple."

"I'm not sure I understand," Jay admitted.

"Lorrie and John urge me to sign the will that gives them this island and everything else I own. I will do so, today. But—" he smiled more broadly— "tomorrow I shall, without their knowing, write another will, by hand. In it I'll say that I was forced to sign the will leaving everything to Lorrie and John. I shall rely on you to mail the new will to my lawyer." He nodded his head with satisfaction. "John and Lorrie won't know that my new, handwritten will, thanks to you, will be in the mail."

Dexter cleared his throat. "But how will we know when it is safe to come back tomorrow? What if Lorrie and John are with you?"

Mr. Whitson pursed his lips. "A signal, that's what we'll need, a signal." Then he smiled again. "I have it! There is a flag, an American flag, that I raise each morning. It is just outside my window. You can see it easily from the channel. If the flag is up, don't row to the island. If the flag is down, you'll know Lorrie and John are in the game room. That is a room attached to the boathouse. They spend hours there every day. When they are there, it will be safe for you to come to me. You can tell by the flag."

Just then a door slammed somewhere in the house, and Mr. Whitson stiffened. "That will be Lorrie, coming to take me away from my retreat and my books. You must not let her see you. All would be lost. Leave at once and keep yourselves hidden."

Jay and Dexter hurriedly got up from their chairs.

"Remember, you must come tomorrow," whispered Mr. Whitson. "It's terribly important. I must give you the letter."

"We'll come, and we'll bring my sister, Cindy," Jay promised.

"Good." Mr. Whitson frowned and waved them away. "Here comes Lorrie. It would be dangerous if she saw you."

The boys ran along the fence to the gate. They

pulled it open and hurried through, then crouched low as they heard someone approach Mr. Whitson in his alcove of pine trees. Through the leaves they could see a young woman wearing a peach-colored silk dress. A silk ribbon of the same color ran through her black hair, which was softly curled and flowed down her back. Pale pink earrings dangled gracefully from her ears. From their hiding place, the boys could smell her flowery perfume. She folded her white arms and looked crossly at Mr. Whitson.

"How many times have I told you not to come wandering down here without letting me know?" the woman demanded. "You absolutely terrify me, Granddad. You could get lost or fall down and break a leg. I'm afraid we're going to have to confine you to the house."

"That, my dear, will never be something to which I subscribe," Mr. Whitson said firmly. "This island is all I have left. I fully intend to use it the way I see fit."

Good for you, Jay thought.

"Well," Lorrie said, "you've been out here long enough now." She reached a slender white arm to the old man. "In now, come on, like a good boy. You'll need a little nap before our business meeting tonight."

The boys saw Mr. Whitson flinch from her touch, but he got up slowly. As soon as Lorrie's back was turned, he stared in Dexter and Jay's direction and winked.

They watched in silence as the old man and Lorrie made their way up to the house.

"He really is a prisoner here on his own island," Jay said, when Lorrie and Mr. Whitson were inside.

"And John and Lorrie are going to take him away tomorrow," added Dexter.

"Unless he signs everything," said Jay.

The boys headed back through the brush and pine trees toward the small beach where they had left Cindy and the rowboat.

But Cindy was nowhere in sight.

"Cindy!" Jay called in a whisper. "Where are you?" She stepped out from behind a tree.

"Oh, I'm so glad you're here," she said with a sigh of relief. "Someone was sneaking around spying on me. I was scared!"

"Who was it?" asked Jay.

"I don't know. It was someone wearing a hat with a large brim. He's gone now, I can tell, but he'll probably be back. Let's get out of here before it's too late!"

"First, we've got to tell you what's happened," Dexter said.

"Later," said Cindy. "After we're in the boat and on our way."

Cindy and the boys headed for the rowboat. Jay untied the anchor, and in a moment they had pushed off. This time Jay was at the oars.

Dexter and Cindy watched the island.

The boys told her about their adventure with Mr. Whitson—about Lorrie and John and Mr. Whitson's daughter Cassie.

"It must have been John who was watching me," said Cindy. "Maybe he's watching us this very minute."

They looked back at the trees and flickering shadows. Jay rowed hard and fast. Soon they were in the protected channel, well out of sight of the island.

"Mr. Whitson just can't believe what Cassie told him in her letter," Jay told Cindy. "He can't believe that she would change so much. So he's going to write a second will leaving everything to Cassie if, but only if, she will keep the island as it is. He is counting on us to mail a letter and the new will to his lawyer."

Cindy frowned. "So we go back to the island tomorrow. We wait in the channel until we're sure the flag is down. That will mean the coast is clear. Then we'll get the envelope from Mr. Whitson, the envelope with the letter for his lawyer and the new, handwritten will."

"Right," said Dexter.

"It sounds easy enough," Cindy said. "I guess nothing can go wrong."

"Maybe," said Dexter. He crossed his fingers.

4 • *Ghosts Around the Campfire?*

As the Spotlighters pulled up close to the boathouse, only Guy was in sight. He was still working on the engine. Dexter tied the boat to the pier while Jay and Cindy climbed out.

Guy looked up and smiled, then rubbed his smudged hands on his jeans and walked toward them. "The tourists have returned, I see. Well, I'm afraid I have a bit of bad news." He scratched the short, reddish stubble on his chin. "Little Mary B. came down with a pain something fierce, and her pa decided to take her home. He couldn't wait for you to get back. He's afraid she might be having an appendicitis attack."

"Oh, no!" Cindy groaned.

"Appendicitis!" said Jay. "She might have to have an operation!"

"It looks as though you three will have to cut short your vacation, too," Guy continued. "Mr. Beech says he'll be back tomorrow by one o'clock to pick you up and take you home." The Spotlighters exchanged worried glances.

"Hey, don't look so upset," Guy said cheerfully. "Mary B. will be all right. And you'll be coming back up here. Mr. Beech said so. As soon as Mary B. is feeling better."

The Spotlighters were still silent, thinking about the island and the old man.

"It's more than just missing a vacation," Cindy said finally. "While we were out exploring, Jay and Dexter met an old man, Mr. Whitson, on an island. Something funny is going on there. Mr. Whitson needs us to help him, but we can't if we're leaving tomorrow."

"He lives on an island that wasn't on the map," Jay said. "There's supposed to be a swamp there, according to the map you gave us." He looked at Guy. "Why didn't you put the island on the map?"

"Ahh, the old man—Mr. Whitson," Guy said, pushing his cap back on his head. "That's a story, kids. I know all the stories around here and all the people. Mr. Whitson is an old, feeble-minded man bent on making trouble for everybody. His grandkids are trying to help him, to protect him."

Guy paused and then went on. "I didn't include the island on the map for the sake of the family's privacy. Curiosity seekers would only create more trouble for them. The old man's always imagining that someone's trying to steal his money and his island." Guy tapped his head. "Feeble-minded fancies, that's what he has. You don't want to get tangled up with Mr. Whitson. No, you'd just upset him, poor soul."

Jay and Dexter frowned.

Guy went on, "I try to help in the only way I know how, making it look on the map as if there's no lake there, no island. Of course, there are always fishermen who find their way into the little channel, just poking about. There's nothing I can do about them. But fishermen only fish, they usually don't land on the island. In fact," Guy looked at the Spotlighters, "you're the only ones so far this year."

He smiled. "I guess it's because kids are curious. Well, now that you know the story, you shouldn't go back there. You wouldn't be welcome, and you'd only aggravate the old man."

The Spotlighters said nothing. Could Mr. Whitson be feeble-minded and confused the way Guy said he was? Cindy wondered. But even if Guy believed that, she could see that Jay and Dexter didn't. And she didn't really, either. Somehow, they'd have to go back to the island in the morning.

"Well, now," said Guy. "A campfire is a sure way to cheer you all up. And with four of us working, we'll have it blazing in a jiffy. Let's go! We can roast the hot dogs that are up there in the Beeches' refrigerator, since we don't have any fish!"

Pushing his cap back on his head, Guy walked over to the sandy clearing where last night's campfire had been. The Spotlighters followed, a few paces behind him.

"Somehow we'll have to make time to get back to Mr. Whitson tomorrow," Cindy said under her breath to Jay.

"We'll leave for the island first thing in the morning," he whispered back.

Ahead of them, Guy was running his foot over the ashes from last night's fire. "Cindy," he called: "You gather pine needles and acorns and dried leaves. Boys, you pick up some twigs and branches. I'll get the dry firewood that's near the house."

The Spotlighters scattered, and in moments they returned with their arms full.

"There's nothing to this fire-making business," Guy said as he expertly arranged first the leaves, acorns, and twigs, then the branches and the logs. In another moment, a fire was burning steadily. The logs crackled and hissed as the flames licked over spots of sap.

"We're ready to cook supper," Guy announced. "Who wants to run up to the cottage and grab the hot dogs?"

"I do," Cindy offered. "I want to call Mrs. Beech, anyway."

While Cindy was gone, Guy showed the boys how to cut and sharpen green, slender twigs from the trees. "No better way to roast a hot dog," he said when he finished. "We'll just put these sticks through the hot dogs the long way—then the meat'll roast evenly."

Cindy returned with the hot dogs and buns and a package of marshmallows. While they all threaded their hot dogs on the sticks, she told about her phone call to Mrs. Beech. "Mary B.'s in the hospital. She had to have her appendix out, but Mrs. Beech said everything went all right. Mary B. will be home in a few days." Cindy paused and looked at the boys.

"But that's not all the news," she said with a smile. "Mr. Beech won't be here to pick us up until three-thirty or four tomorrow."

"Great!" Jay and Dexter said together. The Spotlighters were all thinking the same thing: now they'd have time to get to the island and help Mr. Whitson.

"Am I the only hungry one here?" Guy said, interrupting their thoughts. His hot dog was sizzling over the fire.

"Nope," Dexter said, thrusting his stick into the flames. "I'm ravenous."

"If that means starved, I am, too," Jay said.

After several hot dogs each, the Spotlighters leaned back, their knees clasped between their arms.

"I'm stuffed," Cindy admitted with a sigh.

"Even too stuffed for marshmallows?" Guy chided.

"No way!" Cindy laughed, breaking open the package of marshmallows.

A soft gust of wind shifted the smoke and rustled the leaves in the trees.

"No people in miles," Guy said softly, his voice deep. "Only ghosts." Cindy shivered and moved closer to Jay.

"Some say," Guy went on, "that when the smoke of a campfire is out of sight, it turns into a vengeful spirit that wants to come back to kill the one who took its life."

Cindy hoped Guy would tell them a scary ghost story. She waited for him to go on.

"There are lots of superstitious tales about the north woods. Some night when I have more time I'll tell you a few." Guy rubbed his hands on his jeans and looked at the star-studded sky. "But now the day's gone, and I still have work to do. I've got another project to finish up a couple miles across the lakes. If you need me for anything, my number's in the phone book. Guy Sanderson. I'll be home in an hour or so. Just remember to make sure the fire's out before you turn in," he warned.

Cindy felt a twinge of disappointment that Guy had to leave. The mood was so right for a ghost story: the dark shapes of trees swayed in the gentle breeze, and strange shadows danced across the water and sand. Occasionally a lone owl hooted in the night.

But Guy rose. "Drown the fire with water, choke it with sand, never leave so much as a tiny spark. If a wind came, that spark would turn into a fire, and that fire could get out of control, burning down the whole forest and everything in it."

"We'll be careful," Dexter promised.

The boys and Cindy thanked Guy and watched him as he walked toward the cottage. They heard his truck start up and pull away. Soon all was silent except for the deep croaking of bullfrogs.

The Spotlighters stared without speaking at the dying embers of the fire, each caught up in separate thoughts. Minutes passed, the comfortable silence unbroken except for the gentle lapping of the water and the bullfrogs' croaking.

Cindy lay back on the sand and studied the dark sky. Her thoughts drifted to Mr. Whitson. She could picture him as a boy, lying on the sand, too, staring up at the sky. No wonder he loved this part of the world so much. It was so peaceful and beautiful.

"I could stay here all summer," she sighed.

"So could I," said Jay.

They were quiet for a long time, listening to the leaves whisper in the breeze.

Suddenly Cindy tensed. There was a new sound. She concentrated, closing her eyes. There it was again—a rhythmic splashing.

"Listen," she whispered urgently. It sounded like an oar being dipped in and out of the water.

"There's a boat near here," she said softly.

They listened, but now all was silent.

"Guess not," sighed Cindy. "It's hard to sort out new noises up here."

Dexter leaned forward and adjusted the logs with a stick. The fire hissed and crackled as they watched.

"I wish we could stay longer," Dexter said after a while. "I think Mr. Whitson needs us. He must get awfully lonely up here."

"Whatever we do," Jay said, "we've got to get back to the island tomorrow to help him."

Cindy hunched closer to the boys. In the glow of the fire, their faces were still. There was another sound now—crunching twigs. Something or somebody was in the woods directly behind Cindy.

The Spotlighters drew close together in the dark clearing. Their small fire cast eerie shadows around them. Again there was the sound of crunching twigs and leaves.

"What is it?" Cindy whispered.

"A deer, maybe," Dexter offered. But the footsteps weren't those of a shy, light-footed deer. They were plodding, heavy, and sure.

"Maybe it's John, from the island," whispered Jay.

The Spotlighters froze. Had he followed them when they left the island? If he had, why hadn't they noticed him? Was he now stalking in the woods near them, listening and waiting?

The sound of the steady footsteps grew closer and louder.

"Maybe it's the ghost," Jay said, trying to make a joke. "The ghost that Guy told us about."

"Of course not," Cindy whispered. But she was still thinking about the ghost, herself.

She strained to see into the dark woods but couldn't.

"Let's go back to the house," Jay whispered. He started throwing handfuls of sand on the fire. Dexter and Cindy joined him, and in a minute the fire was out. They started toward the cabin. Then they heard the crackling again. This time it sounded closer.

"Run!" said Dexter.

They burst into the cabin and slammed the door behind them. Without speaking, they went to the big picture window overlooking the beach. They stared out but could see only darkness.

"Someone was there," Cindy said positively. "Someone was watching us and listening."

The boys looked at each other. Who was it— John? They watched and waited. Finally they crawled into their sleeping bags and fell asleep, but they all slept fitfully, tossing and turning.

5 • Buried Letters

CINDY WAS DREAMING that she was shipwrecked on a tiny island with a parrot when a loud pounding on the front door wakened her. She sat up, her heart thumping. Was it morning? Had Mr. Beech come back for them already? She felt as though she hadn't slept at all. Through the window she could see the sky was light. She looked at her watch. Seven o'clock.

"Up and at 'em, rise and shine!" called a voice from outside the door. The Spotlighters pulled themselves out of their sleeping bags. Jay opened the door. There was Guy, a fishing rod slung over his shoulder.

"We've got to get 'em while they're biting," he said cheerfully. "Can't wait for sleepyheads. I thought since your vacation will be cut short, you might at least catch some fish." He looked eagerly at the Spotlighters. "Well? Are you just going to stand there, or get dressed and come with me? I've got doughnuts along for breakfast."

Cindy, Jay, and Dexter looked at each other in dismay. When would they be able to get back to the island? And how could they gracefully turn down Guy's generous offer?

"I promise you'll each catch something to be proud of," Guy went on. "We're going to have forty-five minutes of fishing heaven."

The Spotlighters hesitated. Forty-five minutes? That wasn't so long. They'd still have time to go to the island before Mr. Beech came to pick them up at three-thirty. And how could they refuse when Guy was making a special effort to please them?

"Sounds great," Jay said. "We'll be dressed and down at the pier in five minutes."

"See you there," Guy said cheerfully.

"Let's get going," Jay said to Cindy and Dexter. "The sooner we leave the sooner we'll be back. And the sooner we'll be at the island."

In five minutes the Spotlighters had arranged themselves and their fishing tackle in Guy's big fishing boat. Guy started the engine.

It was a beautiful morning, and Cindy knew that she should have a wonderful time. But she couldn't help thinking about Mr. Whitson. He was counting on Jay and Dexter. They *had* to get back to the island before Mr. Beech came for them.

Guy turned off his engine ten minutes later. "This is the place for walleyes," he told them. "If we don't have a strike soon, we'll head for another spot."

They had scarcely put their lines in the water when something grabbed Dexter's hook. His pole bent over sharply.

"You've got one, Dex!" Jay shouted. "Pull it in."

Dexter let his line play out a little, then jerked his pole up quickly. "Got it," he said excitedly. There was a big splash, and a long fish leaped out of the water.

"A walleye," Guy said admiringly. "A fighter. Keep your line steady and pull it in a bit at a time."

Dexter frowned with concentration and did as Guy directed. His line zigzagged in the water. His pole bent. Behind him Guy said, "Good. I've got the net here."

In the next minute, Guy had leaned over the edge of the boat and scooped up Dexter's walleye. It fought and thrashed in the net, sending columns of spray in every direction.

"Wow!" Dexter said proudly.

"Terrific," Jay said, studying his own fishing pole with more interest now.

Guy showed the Spotlighters how to remove the hook from the fish and put a stringer through its gills.

A moment later, Jay had a strike. But he lost whatever was at the end of his line.

"Better luck next time," Guy said.

There were no more bites. They all sat in silence, watching their lines in the water. Cindy had trouble concentrating.

"We'll have to be getting back," she said finally. "We have a lot to do if we're going to be ready for Mr. Beech."

"Okay," Guy said.

He tried to start the engine, but it sputtered and stalled. He tried again. The engine started up but still sputtered. "This machine just doesn't sound right to me today, kids. I'm afraid we'll have to go over to the marina."

The Spotlighters exchanged worried looks.

"How far is it?" Cindy asked.

"Oh, just a hop, skip, and a jump," Guy told her. "About five lakes as the crow flies."

Cindy frowned. How long would it take to get all the way there and all the way back?

"What's a marina, anyway?" asked Dexter.

"It's a place where people dock their boats," Guy said, heading through a narrow channel. "You can also go there for repairs and gas and supplies. They even sell boats—some pretty fancy ones, too. It's an interesting place, all right."

In other circumstances, the marina would have seemed interesting to the Spotlighters, too. But now going there only meant losing time. They had to get to Mr. Whitson.

The trip to the marina seemed to take forever, but finally they arrived. Guy immediately started talking with a mechanic, and soon the two men were puttering with the engine. Cindy and the boys walked around looking at the many boats— sailboats, fishing boats, float boats, speedboats. There were boats of all shapes and sizes. But the Spotlighters could only think about Mr. Whitson.

At last they heard Guy's voice. "Hey, kids!" he said, beaming. "The boat's all set. We'll have a bite to eat before we take off. My treat."

Dexter looked at Jay and Cindy. What could they do?

"Let's eat fast," Cindy whispered as Guy walked ahead of them into a small, crowded restaurant attached to the marina.

But it was impossible to hurry. There was no room at the counter, and they had to wait for a table. By the time they had been seated and served, another hour had passed. It was already nearly two-thirty. Mr. Beech would be coming for them soon.

The trip back from the marina to the Beeches' pier took over an hour. The Spotlighters' impatience had turned into despair. They thanked Guy for everything as they got their tackle out of his boat.

"Well, I guess you three will be leaving soon," he said. "Nice to have met all of you. When Mr. Beech comes, tell him that I'm over at the Hills' working on a water pump. I'll be back later to take his boat over to the marina for repairs."

The Spotlighters nodded goodbye as Guy roared off in his boat. Then they trudged silently up to the cottage.

"We'll have to make Mr. Beech wait, that's all. We've got to get to the island!" said Jay. "We promised!"

Just as they were nearing the cottage, they heard the telephone ringing. "I'll get it," Cindy said, running ahead.

When she came back outside she was smiling. "Guess what! That was Mr. Beech," Cindy said. "He can't pick us up today, and he wonders if we would mind spending one more day and night here alone. He's been trying to reach us all morning."

Cindy rattled off the rest of Mr. Beech's message. "Mary B.'s fine, don't worry. But Mr. Beech didn't want to leave her since it's the first time Mary B.'s ever had to stay in a hospital. Mr. Beech said he could arrange to have Guy put us on a bus, but he figured we'd rather stay here. He's already called our parents to ask their permission."

"What good luck!" Dexter said, smiling.

"Let's get going," Jay said. "We don't have any time to lose."

Soon the Spotlighters were in the small rowboat heading toward the forgotten island. When they reached the narrow channel, Dexter stopped rowing for a moment.

"Let's hope the flag is down," he said.

Cindy nodded. "What should we do if it's up?"

"Hide and wait," suggested Jay.

Dexter maneuvered the boat through the channel. Then he rested the oars and the Spotlighters peered toward the island.

"The flag is up," groaned Dexter.

"Well, we'll just have to wait," said Jay.

The three of them sat, protected from view by the tall, whispering weeds. "Too bad we can't get out and stretch," said Cindy after a while. "My legs are going to sleep."

"Better your legs than your head," Jay told her. Suddenly he tensed. "Look. The flag's coming down."

Dexter straightened and nodded. "The coast is clear." He rowed quickly toward the island.

"Listen," Jay said as they approached the tiny sand beach. "We know Lorrie and John are out of the way now. But what if they decide to come back to the house? We'd all be there. They'd find us, and then nobody could help Mr. Whitson."

Cindy spoke up. "Jay, why don't you pretend you're fishing? Drop Dexter and me off and circle around the island, then keep an eye on the boathouse. If John and Lorrie leave the game room—"

Jay interrupted Cindy. "I know! I'll do one of my birdcalls. I'll call bobwhite five times if I see them leave."

"We'll listen," Cindy said.

The three Spotlighters rowed close to shore. Dexter and Cindy got out, and Jay moved up to take the oars. He put on an old fishing cap that was at the bottom of the boat.

"Run for the beach if you hear me call," Jay said. "Otherwise I'll pick you up in a half hour."

Cindy and Dexter hurried through the woods. As they approached the screened-in porch, they could see Mr. Whitson standing in the shadows. He must be waiting for us, thought Cindy.

Dexter cleared his throat. "Mr. Whitson? It's Dexter Tate."

Mr. Whitson walked over to the screen door and opened it. "I knew you wouldn't let me down," he said.

They stepped inside, and Dexter introduced Cindy.

"I'm sorry you had to wait so long," Mr. Whitson apologized. "There was no way I could get away from Lorrie and John."

He shook his head. "I signed the will they wanted me to sign, but now they're going to take me away anyway."

"They can't take you away!" cried Cindy. "We won't let them!"

Mr. Whitson smiled at her. "The important thing now is for you to mail this letter and my new will. You'll do that, won't you?"

They nodded. "Of course," Dexter said. He put the envelope in his pocket.

"Keep out of sight. If Lorrie and John knew you were trying to help me, you'd be in grave danger."

"We'll be careful," Cindy promised. They let themselves out of the porch and ran quickly into the yard. In a moment they had come to the fence and the gate.

Dexter opened the gate, and they made their way back to the small beach. Quickly they found shelter in a cluster of bushes.

"We can watch for Jay from here," said Dexter. They pulled some branches around them and sat in silence for a moment.

"We have to do something," Cindy said finally. "We have to keep Lorrie and John from taking Mr. Whitson away from the island."

"Maybe we can think of something when Jay comes," Cindy said. She tilted her head, listening. Just the natural sounds of the woods, she decided. Then she heard the noise again and reached for Dexter's arm. He had heard it, too. They froze, their hearts pounding. A crackling in the woods. Like the sounds they had heard the night before. Someone was nearby. Could it be John?

After Jay had dropped Cindy and Dexter at the small beach, he rowed around the island. He stopped when he had a view of the boathouse.

He put the oars inside the boat and got his

fishing pole ready. After all, he was supposed to look like a fisherman. He reached into his carton of worms and felt around until he found one. It was lucky worms couldn't feel, he thought, as he pushed the hook through the slimy body. He lowered the hook into the water, then settled back against the orange life preserver, watching his red bobber drift in the blue water.

Jay thought about Mr. Whitson and Cassie. Why didn't she write to him? Or come to see him? It was very strange that she wanted to turn this peaceful island into a noisy, crowded tourist resort. From what Mr. Whitson had said about Cassie, she loved the island as much as he did. Jay sighed. She must love money more. The chance to sell the island to some promoters was too tempting to her. He didn't blame Mr. Whitson for being disappointed. He wouldn't blame him if he gave the island to John and Lorrie.

Suddenly Jay's pole jerked and bent. He pulled the line up fast, anticipating a large fish. But there was only a weed on the end. Feeling silly, he pulled off the weed and lowered the hook into the water again.

The sun was getting lower in the sky. Late afternoon was a good time for fishing, Guy had said. Jay cast a few more times. Then his hook caught on something again, making his pole bend sharply toward the water. He tugged at his pole, but nothing pulled back. He hadn't caught a fish. He was snagged on a log, probably. He jerked his line, but it stayed taut.

Jay reeled in the line, slowly pulling the rowboat over to the place where the line entered the water.

His hook was really caught tight. He tugged gently and a cloud of mud appeared. He tugged a little more. Then he leaned over and reached into the water. What was he caught on, anyway?

He followed the submerged line with his hand

until he reached a rope tied around something—something soft and slippery. His hook had caught a loop of heavy cord that was wrapped about a slimy bag of some kind.

Reaching deeper into the water, he followed the cord with his fingers. The water was up to his shoulder, and the boat was beginning to tip. The bag must be tied to a rock or something. It had been very well hidden, but not well enough.

He reached in his pocket for his jackknife and cut the cord that connected the slimy package to the rock. Then he hauled the bag into the boat.

Jay looked at it, frowning. It was a canvas bag. It had been left here so that someone could come back for it. What a strange hiding place!

What was in the bag? Jay felt the wet canvas. Maybe this wasn't any of his business. But maybe it was. He examined the heavy cord that was tied around the bag. There were many double knots, each tied thoroughly and expertly. His heart pounded as he cut the final knot.

The opening of the bag was fastened with large snaps. Jay pulled them apart and reached inside. Another bag, this one plastic. A package within a package. He could feel a box inside—a large metal box.

Was there money in the box? Jay looked up to find that the boat had drifted close to the island. Anyone who was looking could see exactly what he had found and what he was doing.

He set the plastic bag down and took up the oars. He turned the boat around and rowed away from shore. He could only hope that no one had seen him.

There. Now he was a good distance out. He'd have to watch to make sure he didn't drift in again.

The plastic bag was fastened at the top with a tight, wet knot. Taking out his knife again, Jay split the plastic, reached inside, and withdrew the metal box.

There were two clasps. Taking a deep breath, Jay opened one, then the other. He raised the lid.

Inside, there were several packets, each neatly wrapped in small clear plastic bags. The packets contained envelopes. Was money inside them? Should he wait to open them until he'd rowed back to Dexter and Cindy? Jay bit his lip. No, he'd have to look now. If John and Lorrie had been watching, they'd be waiting for him to come back to the island. They'd take the box before he could find out what was inside.

Jay slit the plastic and lifted out a packet of envelopes. The envelopes were tied together with string, and the string had been fastened with double knots—the way the rope around the canvas bag had been fastened.

Turning the small package over in his hands, Jay saw that the top one was addressed to Mr. Whitson. He cut the string so that he could see the rest of the letters.

Alan Whitson…Alan Whitson…Alan Whitson! The postmark was Los Angeles. And the name on the back, with the return address, was Cassie Underhill.

Jay's heart pounded. These were letters that Cassie had written to Mr. Whitson—letters that Mr. Whitson had never seen!

He looked through the rest of the stack. The other envelopes were addressed to Cassie. And the return address was Alan Whitson's. The letters Mr. Whitson had written to Cassie had never been mailed!

Jay thrust the bag of letters under the seat. Cassie hadn't let Mr. Whitson down, after all. Jay could picture the old man's face when he heard the news.

He looked at his watch. Almost twenty minutes had gone by since he'd left Jay and Cindy at the beach. It was time to row back for them. He could hardly wait to tell them what he'd found.

Lorrie and John must have typed the letter Mr. Whitson received from Cassie. They must have forged her signature. They had tried to trick Mr. Whitson so that he would change his will—so that he would give them the island. For a moment, Jay wondered why they hadn't destroyed the letters, instead of hiding them there. It seemed strange.

As he came near the island, Jay glanced over his shoulder and stared. A man wearing a wide-brimmed hat and a beard was standing on the beach. He was holding a rifle. It must be John, Jay thought.

And then the man slowly raised the rifle to his shoulder and aimed it at Jay.

6 • Man with a Gun

DEXTER AND CINDY sat tensely, waiting for Jay to row in to shore. How could they warn him that John was standing nearby, watching him? It could be no one else, they were sure.

Was John going to try to keep them from leaving the island? Dexter felt the envelope in his pocket. Did John know Mr. Whitson had given him a new will? Did John suspect that they were trying to help Mr. Whitson?

Cindy leaned forward. "Here comes Jay," she whispered. She could see her brother rowing steadily, looking over his shoulder at the beach.

A shot rang out. Cindy screamed as Jay fell backwards into the rowboat.

There was another shot and another. Stumbling, Cindy started toward the beach, Dexter on her heels.

"Jay, Jay," Cindy could scarcely speak, her voice caught in her throat.

Dexter grabbed her arm. "Careful!" he warned. "He's still shooting!"

Cindy pulled away and kept running, her eyes on the rowboat. She fell, bruising her elbow. When Dexter helped her up they saw that the man was aiming his rifle up at the sky.

Dexter and Cindy looked again at the rowboat, and Cindy trembled with relief. Jay was sitting up.

Another explosion ripped through the air. Jay grabbed the oars and pulled the boat in to shore. Cindy and Dexter dragged the boat up onto the sand and helped Jay climb out.

"I'm all right," Jay said, his voice shaky.

Dexter turned angrily to John. "You could have killed him!"

"This is no place for you kids," John said.

"Why are you shooting, anyway?" Cindy asked, so angry she could hardly talk.

"I hate pests, pests that haunt this island. Crows. Starlings. Squirrels. Pests, all of them."

Cindy stared at the rifle.

John narrowed his pale blue eyes at her, his thumb tapping the butt of the gun. "I missed that crow, the one that was flying just above your head," he said to Jay.

Jay knew there had been no crow. He said nothing, but stared angrily at John.

"I want all three of you off this island now," John said. "And I mean it." His thumb still tapped the butt of his rifle. "This is private property. You don't belong here. Got that? Now move."

He pointed the gun at the rowboat. Jay and Cindy got into the boat without a word. Dexter shoved away from shore and hopped in himself.

Maybe John hadn't seen him find the letters, after all, Jay thought as he rowed toward the channel.

"I've never been so scared in my whole life," Cindy finally said in a whisper. "I thought he'd shot you."

"So did I," Jay admitted. "I threw myself down so he wouldn't have a sitting target."

"He's a dangerous man," said Dexter.

"As soon as we get out of sight, I've got something to show you," Jay said. "Something I found in the lake. Letters. Letters that Cassie's written to Mr. Whitson, that John and Lorrie never showed him. And letters that he's written to her, that John and Lorrie never mailed."

Cindy gasped. "Then they've been tricking Mr. Whitson, trying to get him to believe that Cassie doesn't care about him anymore!"

Dexter took off his glasses and polished them on his shirt. "What about that letter Mr. Whitson showed us? The letter that Cassie signed?"

"I'm sure John and Lorrie typed it and forged her name," Jay said. He guided the boat into the narrow channel until they were surrounded by the sheltering reeds. John couldn't see them now. Jay put the oars inside the boat, then pulled the bag out from under the seat. He opened the bag and showed the letters to Dexter and Cindy.

"We've got to tell Mr. Whitson," Jay said. "Before he signs the deed and the will."

"He already signed it," Dexter said. "But John and Lorrie are going to take him away, anyway."

"We have the new will and the letter he wrote to his lawyer," Cindy said. "But we still have to tell him about the letters you found. He needs to know that Cassie didn't let him down after all."

Suddenly they heard something. A motor. A boat was coming from the island. It couldn't be anyone but John. Was he coming for them?

Quickly Jay reached for the oars. Maybe they could hide in the tall reeds.

"They might be taking Mr. Whitson away with them now," said Dexter.

Jay pulled the boat farther into the reeds, and they ducked down as the noise of the motorboat drew nearer. The engine slowed as it neared the opening of the channel. The Spotlighters held their breaths.

As soon as they heard the boat pass them, Dexter looked up. "It's John, and he's alone," he said. They watched until the motorboat was out of sight.

"At least we know Mr. Whitson's still on the island," said Jay.

"With Lorrie," added Dexter.

"I'm not afraid of Lorrie," Cindy declared.

"Let's go back to the island while John's gone. At least we can find a way to tell Mr. Whitson about Cassie. That's the important thing." She hesitated. "But if John comes back, and they try to take Mr. Whitson away—"

Jay interrupted. "We need help. I'll go to the Beeches' and call the police. You stay on the island and tell Mr. Whitson about the letters. John will never know you're there. But we've got to hurry. We don't know how long he'll be gone."

He grabbed the oars and started rowing back to the island.

When the rowboat neared land, Jay handed Cindy the canvas bag with the letters. "Show these to Mr. Whitson. I'll be back as fast as I can."

"While you're gone, mail this," Dexter said, giving Jay the envelope addressed to Mr. Whitson's lawyer.

Dexter and Cindy climbed out of the boat as it touched the shore.

Jay put the letter in his pants pocket. Then he turned the boat around and headed away from the island once more. When he glanced over his shoulder, there was no sign of Cindy and Dexter.

He rowed as fast as he could, but it seemed to take forever just to reach the channel. What if he met John on the way to the Beeches'? He hadn't thought of that. John would see that he was alone and would guess that the others were on the island.

Jay tried to row faster, but he was getting tired. His hands were already blistered, and his back ached. It was nearly twilight. The trip from the island to the Beeches' hadn't seemed this far before.

He tried to think of what he'd say when he called the police. Should he say that someone was being held against his will? Should he try to explain about the letters? What would be the quickest way to get the police to the island?

"Hurry," he whispered to himself each time he dipped the oars in the water. "Hurry!"

There. At last he could see Mr. Beech's boathouse. He was only a moment from the telephone. And the police.

As he rowed closer, he saw that the door of the boathouse was open. Someone was inside. His heart pounded. Could John be there, waiting?

Then Jay saw that a boat was tied up at the dock, and he breathed a sigh of relief. It was Guy's boat. There was the sound of a drill coming from the boathouse. Guy must be working on Mr. Beech's boat.

Jay brought the rowboat alongside the dock and climbed out. He tied the boat loosely to one of the posts, and decided he'd better tell Guy what was going on. Maybe Guy could help. Of course. He could take Jay and the police back to the island in his boat.

He ran into the boathouse. "Guy!" he shouted over the sound of the drill.

Guy turned around, shutting off the drill at the same time. When he saw Jay he took a step back. "What are you doing here?" he asked.

"We found something—"

Guy interrupted. "What are you doing here?" he asked again. "Where's Mr. Beech?"

Jay shook his head. It seemed as if the telephone call from Mr. Beech had happened long ago. "He couldn't come. But, Guy—while I was fishing, I found some letters. They'd been carefully wrapped and hidden in the lake. A whole batch of them. Letters that Mr. Whitson's daughter Cassie had written to him and letters he had written to her. His granddaughter Lorrie and her husband have tricked Mr. Whitson into signing everything he owns over to them!"

Jay hoped Guy would understand quickly so they could call the police right away.

Jay took a deep breath. "Mr. Whitson's signed a will leaving the island and everything else to Lorrie and John. He signed it so they wouldn't take him away where Cassie couldn't find him. But they're going to take him away anyway!"

Guy's face drained white under the stubble. He stared at Jay. "So the old man signed. When?"

"Last night, maybe this morning. We've got to do something fast. He's afraid they're going to take him away!"

Guy set his drill on a ledge and sat down. "Letters. You found the letters in the lake?"

Jay nodded. "Lorrie and John never mailed the letters Mr. Whitson wrote to Cassie telling her that he was on the island. And they never gave him the letters she wrote to him! They've lied to him. They've tricked him into leaving them everything that he owns!"

"Where are the letters now?" asked Guy.

He looks angry, Jay thought. Of course, Guy probably was as shocked about the letters and about the cheating as the Spotlighters were. He'd known Mr. Whitson and his family for a long time. No wonder he was upset.

"I left them over on the island with Cindy and Dexter. I'm going back there with the police," Jay said. "Maybe you could take us over in your boat."

"Do Lorrie and John know you have the letters?" Guy asked. His face was still white.

"Oh, no, of course not," said Jay. "If they knew, I'd never have left Cindy over there. Or Dexter. Nobody knows but us."

Guy was silent. He wiped his hands on his blue jeans.

What was Guy waiting for, anyway? Why was he moving so slowly? Suddenly Jay was very aware of the sound of water lapping against the dock. Well, he'd have to call the police now. He'd wasted far too much time already.

As Jay started toward the boathouse door, Guy shifted his position, and Jay saw that he had been sitting on a large box. It had been tied with strong cord that had been fastened with double knots. They looked just like the knots that were on the canvas bag!

Jay stared at the knots and blinked. Had Mr. Beech tied them?

Suddenly he knew.

Guy.

It was Guy who had tied the knots on this box, and it was Guy who had tied the knots on the package in the water. Guy. Not Lorrie, not John. It was Guy who had hidden the letters, who had tied the bag to a rock in the lake.

7 • *Blackmail*

JAY FORCED HIMSELF to look at Guy and to speak calmly. "Would you check the rowboat to make sure I've tied it up okay?" he said. "I'm going up to the cottage."

As he spoke, he knew it was no use. Guy stood up and stepped forward, reached out with both arms, and pushed Jay, hard, against the wall of the boathouse. Guy quickly stepped outside and slammed down the overhead door.

Jay was trapped in the dark boathouse.

"Okay. We understand each other, I think," Guy was saying on the other side of the door.

"Let me out," Jay shouted. He was angry at Guy and angry, too, that he had been so stupid—that he had told Guy about the letters. Why hadn't he suspected that Guy was involved in this whole thing with Lorrie and John?

"No, I won't let you out, not yet. I've got to get those letters, and I've got to get the will. Then I'll think about letting you out of here."

Jay tried to remember how much he had told Guy. Did he know that Cindy had the letters?

Guy's next words made Jay's heart sink. "Your sister's got the letters, right? And she's on the island with your friend Dexter. I'm going over there, and I'm going to get the letters. As long as I get them, your sister won't be in any danger."

Cindy in danger! Jay saw red. "You let me out of here," he shouted.

"If you want your sister to be safe, you tell me everything you know, buddy," said Guy on the other side of the boathouse door.

Jay put his left hand up to his mouth. He bit hard on the knuckle of his index finger to try to pull himself together. No matter what happened, he couldn't let Guy harm Cindy.

"It's the way I told you," Jay said. He was surprised that his voice sounded so calm. "I found the canvas bag with the letters while I was fishing near the island. I told Cindy and Dexter. We decided—" He drew a breath. "We decided that we couldn't handle everything alone. Lorrie and John would keep us from Mr. Whitson. They'd know we were on to them if we tried to force our way in. They might hurt Mr. Whitson. They might hurt Cindy. John has a gun." Thinking about it made Jay close his eyes. "We decided that I should come back and call the police."

"So when you left, maybe half an hour or so ago, Lorrie and John knew nothing about the letters, right, chum?"

"Right," said Jay, taking a deep breath.

"Remember, if you lie to me, and I find out, your sister's in trouble. Serious trouble."

"I'm not lying," said Jay. He slumped down, his back against the wall of the boathouse.

There was a silence. "No use yelling for help, no one's around," said Guy from the other side of the big door. "Let's understand each other. There's nothing you can do. Nothing."

Jay gritted his teeth. Guy was right. There was nothing he could do.

"I've worked a long time on this deal—ever since I found those letters in the desk. Lorrie and John may call it blackmail, but I call it clever. I'm going to get my share. Nothing's going to get in my way now. Nothing and no one—especially not three kids.

"I heard you talking last night around the campfire," Guy went on. "You think you're pretty smart, but you can't fool me. Why do you think I tried to keep you away from the island this morning, anyway?"

Hatred for Guy rose in Jay's throat. So Guy was the person they'd heard in the woods last night—not John. They'd told Guy about meeting Mr. Whitson. Guy must have come back to the cottage to spy on them, to find out more. Then he must have planned the fishing trip to keep them from going back to the island. Probably he had faked the engine trouble.

"Okay, then, sit tight," Guy said. "I'm going over to the island."

Guy's voice seemed farther away now. Jay realized he was walking down the dock to his boat.

Soon the motor started up. As waves lapped against the boathouse, the sound of the engine gradually faded away.

Jay's thoughts reeled. He had to get out, he *would* get out. But how? Guy was on the way over to the island now, on the way to Cindy and Dexter. He'd give them some story about coming alone. They wouldn't know he was a crook. They'd have confidence in him, they'd believe him. They'd have no reason not to.

Jay felt in his pocket. It was lucky Dexter had given him the new will and letter to mail. Cindy and Dexter might have given them to Guy.

By now the sun was going down outside. It was dark in the locked boathouse.

Jay felt around cautiously. He knew there was a door on the far side of the boathouse—a big wooden door that was rarely opened. He remembered seeing a rusted padlock on the outside latch. Maybe the padlock was rusted through and weak. He stepped carefully over the wooden planking and reached the other end of the boathouse. There was the door. Jay could see a faint line of light along one side.

Leaning against the door, he shoved with his

shoulder. The boards shuddered against his weight. Jay heard the thumping of the rusty padlock against the weather-beaten wood. But the door only shook, it did not open. Jay tried again and again. The padlock held firm. In exasperation he kicked at the door, but still the lock did not give. He would never escape the boathouse this way.

The water inside the boathouse lapped against the padded runners that hoisted boats out of the water. Jay was careful to keep his footing away from the dark cavern of water. He moved along the side, feeling for the high windows he had seen boarded up from the outside. There, he found them. He pushed and pounded each window, but they were all stuck shut.

There was nothing he could do. Jay sat down and leaned against the wall of the boathouse. He couldn't get out. He was locked in, unable to get to Dexter and Cindy. And Mr. Whitson. Yelling wouldn't do any good. There was no one near.

His heart was racing. He drew his knees up to his chest and tried to stay calm, to think. But it was hard, knowing that he was trapped in the dark, a prisoner in the boathouse.

Jay put his head between his knees. He'd really made a mess of things. If only he hadn't told Guy about the letters he'd found! Guy had hidden them in the lake. Had he hidden them from Mr. Whitson? Or from John and Lorrie? Blackmail. Guy had used that word.

What else had Guy said? He'd found the letters

in the desk. He must have been snooping around over there on the island when Lorrie and John were gone. When he'd found the letters in the desk, he'd realized that Lorrie and John had hidden them from Mr. Whitson—that they were trying to make him believe that Cassie wasn't interested in him any longer.

Jay stood up restlessly. That was it. Guy had found the letters and had hidden them, threatening to show them to Mr. Whitson unless—unless what? Jay started to pace back and forth.

Without the letters, Guy had no hold over John and Lorrie. With them, he could threaten to show the letters to Mr. Whitson—unless they gave him money. That was it! Blackmail—Guy had said the word himself. He wanted to be paid off. But now that Mr. Whitson had signed the will and Cindy had the letters, Guy had lost his power over Lorrie and John. He wasn't going to get anything. No wonder he was upset!

Jay swallowed. He tried to picture what was happening right now on the island. What had Guy told Cindy and Dexter? They were in danger. And Jay couldn't warn them!

8 • Escape

WHEN JAY DROPPED Cindy and Dexter at the island, they ran from the little beach into the shelter of the trees. They couldn't take a chance on John's seeing them when he came back.

"I want to tell Mr. Whitson about the letters," said Cindy. "Right now."

Dexter shook his head. "I don't think we should. It's almost dark, and Lorrie will be in the house. We can't risk having her see us," he said. "We'll have to wait till Jay comes back with the police."

Cindy nodded. "I guess so," she agreed reluctantly. "I wonder how long it will take Jay to get the police. It gets dark so early in the woods."

They settled down to wait. Within half an hour

they heard a motorboat coming through the channel. "Jay can't be back yet," whispered Dexter. "It must be John. He'll take his boat around to the other side of the island to dock it."

They watched through the trees as John guided the boat out of the channel. He opened up the throttle and sped toward the island. In a moment he was out of sight, on his way to the other side.

"I wonder what he'd do if he knew we were here," whispered Dexter. Cindy shivered. They listened as the sound of the motor faded away.

"As soon as it's really dark, I'll try to disable his boat," Dexter told Cindy. "We've got to make sure he and Lorrie can't get Mr. Whitson away from here."

Cindy leaned against a tree. "I feel so helpless, just sitting here. Hurry up, Jay. Hurry up, police."

The moments dragged. "There's a star," whispered Cindy. "Starlight, starbright, first star I've seen tonight, I wish I may, I wish I might, have the wish I wish tonight." She closed her eyes for a moment.

"What was your wish?" asked Dexter.

"If you tell a wish, it doesn't come true," Cindy

reminded him. "But I can give you a hint. It has to do with Mr. Whitson and Cassie and the island and living happily ever after."

They sat quietly, watching for Jay.

"I hear something," Dexter said at last. He looked again toward the channel. "A boat," he said excitedly. "It's Jay, with the police."

Cindy jumped to her feet. It was hard to make out more than an outline in the growing darkness. "No, it's Guy," she said, surprised. "No Jay, no police."

Dexter squinted. "You're right," he agreed, frowning. "I wonder what he wants. Let's wave him in."

They hurried to the small beach. Guy was already waving to them. Dexter ran over to the boat as it neared shore and helped pull it close enough so that Guy could jump out.

"Jay told me everything," said Guy quickly. "First, give me the letters. Fast."

"They're over here," said Dexter, grabbing the canvas bag from behind a bush.

"Good," said Guy. "Now we've got to hurry. We've got to get the will the old man's signed. We've got to keep it from John and Lorrie. Now that Mr. Whitson's signed it, they'll own everything."

"Where's Jay?" asked Cindy. "And the police?"

"They'll be along shortly," said Guy. "We figured this plan would work best. I've known Lorrie and John for a long time. They trust me. They don't know that the letters have been found. Jay and I talked this all over with the police. I'm to keep Lorrie and John busy down at the dock while you get the will. I know where it is. But we've got to hurry. The police'll want the will when they get here, see? If Lorrie and John see the police coming, they might— well, they might do something foolish. They might harm Mr. Whitson."

Cindy shuddered.

Guy looked at his watch. "Okay. Here's the plan. I'll take my boat over to the dock on the other side of the island where John keeps his. I'll arrive at the house, all smiles, and tell John and Lorrie I want to show them something that's wrong about their boat. There's nothing wrong with it, of course. But they don't know that. I can keep them down there at the dock talking while you get the will."

He placed the bag with the letters in his boat.

"Wait ten minutes. Then get over to the house. You'll hear us go down to the dock. Watch for my signal from the pier. I'll flash my flashlight three times when it's safe for you to go in. I can tell Lorrie and John I'm just testing it. Or looking for bats! Lorrie's scared to death of them."

He took a deep breath. "The will's in the basement in a little workroom. There's a desk there. Look in the bottom right drawer, toward the back. The will's in a brown manilla envelope marked PERSONAL. I know that's where they keep it."

"What shall we do after we find it?" asked Dexter, nervously.

"I'll give you a few minutes, then I'll come up for the envelope. I'll meet you in the front hallway. I'll see that Lorrie and John stay at the dock. The police will be here by that time. We'll have the will and the letters for them."

"What about Mr. Whitson?" asked Cindy.

"We won't tell him anything until the police have Lorrie and John in hand. If he got wind of our plan, he might get upset and wreck it."

"But what if he's there when we go inside the house?" asked Cindy.

"He won't be. He's in his room. He'll stay in there. They've put a latch on the outside, just to keep him from wandering around. They're afraid he'll fall."

"But locking him in his room—that's terrible!" said Cindy.

"Well, it wouldn't be Cassie's way, and soon he'll be with her, right?" Guy paused a moment and looked at Cindy and Dexter. "Now, let's go."

As Guy got into his boat and started the motor, Cindy and Dexter watched.

"Lucky we've got him on our side," said Dexter. "We'll need every bit of help we can get."

Jay wasn't sure how long he had been sitting in the dark boathouse. Twenty minutes? Half an hour? It was hard to tell in the dark. He knew only that the sun had set all the way now. There were no more slivers of light coming through the cracks.

In the north woods night noises were different from day noises, he thought. Bullfrogs croaked in unison. An occasional owl hooted. And the water seemed to lap more loudly against the boathouse frame. The water lapped more loudly inside the boathouse, too, Jay noticed. At least, it seemed louder.

Jay's mouth dropped open. The water *inside* the boathouse was coming from the lake *outside* the boathouse. Of course. When a boat came into the boathouse onto the runners, it never left the water.

Jay slapped his hand against his forehead. "How could I have been so dumb?" he asked out loud. The boathouse was just a shell, protection for the boat against rain and wind. But underneath the runners was lake water. If there was a way for the water to come inside, there was a way for it to leave, as well. And a way for Jay to leave, too. He could swim under the big overhead door!

Eagerly, Jay crawled to the edge of the dark cavern of water. He started to untie his shoes, then thought better of it. He'd save time if he left them on. It wasn't going to be a long swim.

Suddenly he remembered the new will. He couldn't risk getting it wet. He felt around for a hiding place. There—a rock. He'd put the envelope under the rock and come back for it later.

Jay stuck his legs in gingerly first, testing for any obstacles. Then he slid into the water. It was freezing. He swam to the door, then took a deep breath and dove under. In a moment he burst through the surface with a gasp. He was free.

Jay swam slowly to shore. When he got to the beach, he stood up and caught his breath. The night air felt cool on his wet body. Standing in the soft sand, he looked around the black lake.

He would have to hurry. Guy had surely reached the island by now. There was no time to waste. There wasn't even time to call the police.

In the dark, it was almost impossible to see anything. Jay squinted his eyes, trying to make out the rowboat. There it was, tied to the dock. He went over to it and got in.

He felt around for the flashlight. Where was it? He had seen it in the boat earlier. He *had* to have the flashlight. How else could he hope to reach the island in the pitch blackness? But there it was, at the front of the boat. Jay switched it on, and the beam shone strongly in front of him. Too strongly? Would someone on the island be able to see him approach? He couldn't take the chance.

Using a rag he found under the seat of the boat, Jay made a makeshift shield over the head of the flashlight and flicked it on again. Perfect, he thought. The light was bright enough for Jay to see just ahead of him, but faint enough, he was sure, so that it wouldn't be noticed from a distance.

Jay held the flashlight between his knees. He slowly turned the boat around and headed in the direction of the island. He would have to row backwards, he realized, to have the flashlight shining in front of him instead of in back. No matter. He quickly shifted his position and plunged the oars into the water.

He was on his way, the small boat gliding smoothly and evenly across the still, black lake. The only sounds were the splashing of the oars and the gentle creaking of the oarlocks.

After a while Jay stopped rowing and tried to get his bearings. The shoreline looked quite different at night. The usual landmarks were invisible, and the dark shapes of trees seemed to loom larger than they did in the day. Fortunately, scattered lights from a few cabins helped show the way, and Jay knew that he had to turn right about halfway between the first cabin and the last.

He began rowing again, chilled to the bone. He

checked the land on his left. There. He was about
halfway to the island. He swung the boat to the
right and, directing the light from the muffled
flashlight ahead of him, moved slowly forward. The
island lay straight ahead, he was sure.

An owl hooted nearby. Then something small
flapped close by Jay's head, and he ducked. He
heard a small squeaking noise. Was it a bat? But
bats, he knew, rarely attacked people. And they used
their finely developed sense of radar to avoid
contact. They're probably just as scared of me as I
am of them, he thought. But he rowed faster and
crouched down lower in the boat.

Jay was nearing the channel, he could tell. He wiped his blistered hands on his jeans and took a deep breath. In a few minutes he was in the channel, with only a few hundred yards to go to the island. As quickly as he could he guided the rowboat forward.

In a few minutes he stopped rowing and shone his muted flashlight around him. Hundreds of long, graceful reeds nodded back at him. He had arrived at the island. He rowed in to the tiny beach and pulled the boat up on shore.

Jay realized he would have to use his flashlight to get close to the house. He'd never find his way without light. He'd just make sure he kept the beam directed at the ground.

He started toward the house. Where were Dexter and Cindy? Had Guy got the letters from them? What would Guy tell them? What would he do to them?

Shivering in his wet clothes, Jay knew he had to hurry. He had to find Dexter and Cindy. Now.

9 • Jay's Trick

JAY STOPPED TO listen for voices. He heard nothing but caught a glimmer of light ahead. Cautiously, he shut off his flashlight and crept closer. Pine needles crackled beneath his feet. Then he saw the high chain-link fence. He breathed a sigh of relief. All he had to do was follow the fence around to the gate.

It was hard to judge where the gate was in the dark. He remembered that he and Dexter had turned at least one corner. Maybe two. He'd know the gate when he came to it, he was sure.

In a few minutes he felt a gap between two iron

posts. He fumbled for the padlock. The gate swung open without a squeak. Jay carefully headed toward the grove of trees that was Mr. Whitson's favorite reading place. He stuck his flashlight into his belt so he could put both hands in front of him to feel his way.

Suddenly he banged into the small table that he and Dexter had sat at with the old man. Something crashed against the metal and broke. Jay felt the blood rush to his face.

The sound echoed in the night air. Now he would be caught. He knew it. He must have knocked over the lemonade pitcher and broken it. He couldn't stay here—someone from the house might decide to come down and take a look.

He headed toward the house, staying close to the shrubbery. Still the yard was silent. No lights came toward him, no voices shouted. Had no one heard him?

And then he heard a voice, a hoarse whisper, "I'm sure it was just a raccoon."

"But there *are* bears up here. Mary B. told me so."

Jay's heart skipped a beat. Dexter and Cindy!

They were all right, after all. And they were alone. Guy was nowhere to be seen.

"Dex! Cindy!" Jay whispered.

"Oh!" Cindy gasped when she saw Jay. "You scared me—" She stared at him. "Did you bring the police? What happened? How did you get so wet?"

"Shh-sh," Jay interrupted her. He gently laid a hand on her arm. "Where is Guy?"

"He's inside," Dexter said. "He's going to take John and Lorrie down to the dock while we—"

Jay spoke quickly. "Guy locked me in the boathouse. I had to swim underneath it to get out."

"Guy locked you in!" whispered Cindy. "But he's helping us! We have a plan." She paused. "When he gives us the signal, Dex and I are supposed to sneak into the house and get the will. Why did he lock you in the boathouse?"

"Did you call the police?" asked Dexter.

Jay shook his head. "No, there wasn't time. I wanted to get here right away. Guy lied to you. And me. And everybody. It was Guy who hid the letters in the lake. I think he wanted to blackmail Lorrie and John into giving him money. Without those letters, they won't have to give him a thing. When Guy found out that I knew about the letters and everything else, he couldn't take any chances. So he locked me in the boathouse."

"He told us you would be coming to the island later with the police," Cindy said. She looked at Jay and his wet clothes. Anger welled up inside her.

Dexter took a breath. "We gave Guy the letters when he came."

"What about the signal you just mentioned?" Jay asked.

"He'll flash a light from the pier. Three times," Cindy said. "And then he'll keep Lorrie and John down there while we get the will. Guy said he'd make up an excuse about having to show them something that's wrong with their boat."

"And then," Dexter went on, "while they're gone we're supposed to sneak into the house and get the will and hand it over to Guy."

Jay frowned. "So he can keep blackmailing John and Lorrie."

"He didn't count on your escaping from the boathouse," said Cindy.

"We've got to do something," Jay said. "And fast. We've got to get Mr. Whitson away from here."

He bit his lower lip, thinking.

"I've got a plan," he said carefully. "It's risky, but it's the only choice we've got now. We'll sneak Mr. Whitson out of the house and get him to the rowboat. And we'll let Guy believe that his plan is still working—that you're doing exactly as he says about getting the will."

He paused and then went on. "Guy thinks I'm still locked up in the boathouse and that the two of you are without a boat. He also thinks you believe him. You'll give him some papers—but not the right ones."

Dexter and Cindy nodded appreciatively.

"Blank papers will do the trick, at least for a little while," Jay said. "We'll give Guy the envelope, but I'll put old paper inside it instead of the will. We'll give the will to Mr. Whitson. He can destroy it when we've got him safe."

"We're going to have to work fast," Cindy said, looking toward the pier.

"As soon as the light flashes, we'll start," Jay said. "Dex, you can exchange the papers, all right?"

Dexter nodded. "Guy told me where to look in the basement. I'll get the will."

Jay nodded. "Cindy and I will get Mr. Whitson out of the house and down to the rowboat. Dex, you'll give the fake papers to Guy. Then you'll have to get away and meet me at the gate. You'll give me the real papers. I'll take them down to Mr. Whitson and Cindy. Then they can get away in the rowboat."

"But what about you two?" asked Cindy. "I won't leave you here with John and Guy and Lorrie!" Suddenly her face lit up. "Dexter, you know how to run Guy's boat. You watched everything this morning on our fishing trip. You and Jay can escape in it!"

Dexter grinned. "Okay. As soon as I give Guy the false papers, I'll figure out a way to stay out of his sight. He knows or thinks that I can't run away. I'll disable John's boat. And I'll get Guy's boat and bring it around to the little beach, Jay, and pick you up. That way John and Lorrie and Guy can't escape. Then we'll all meet at the Beeches'!"

"What about Guy and John? They'll see you!" worried Cindy.

"I'll think of something," said Dexter quickly, not wanting to think about it.

Cindy grabbed Jay's arm. "Look. The signal!"

From the pier a light flashed three times. It was time to act.

"Now," Jay said urgently. The three detectives hurried to the house. Once inside, Dexter ran to the basement stairs. Jay and Cindy stood in the hallway.

"Where's Mr. Whitson's room?" Jay asked Cindy in a whisper.

Cindy glanced up the stairs and shook her head. "I don't know."

"Let's find it," Jay whispered. "Fast."

They reached the top of the stairs quickly. Ahead of them was a long hallway with three closed doors on each side. "You take the left side, and I'll take the right," Jay whispered.

Cindy nodded and crept along the hall to the first door on the left. Carefully she turned the doorknob and eased the door open. A bathroom. She closed the door quietly and moved down the hallway.

Jay opened a closet door. Then he hurried down the hall and gently opened another door. He smelled perfume and saw a peach-colored dress spread across a bed. This must be Lorrie and John's room.

"Here, Jay!" Cindy whispered. Jay hurried to

the last door on the left. It was latched on the outside. They unlatched the door and opened it quietly. Mr. Whitson was sitting in an old rocking chair. A book was spread open on his lap. He was asleep.

"We don't want to scare him," Jay warned.

Cindy nodded. She gently touched the old man's shoulder and spoke his name softly. "Mr. Whitson—it's us, Jay and Cindy Temple."

Mr. Whitson blinked open his eyes and shook his head in surprise. "What on earth are you doing here?" he exclaimed. "My first visitors in my house since I've been here!" He smiled and shook his head again. "I can't imagine that Lorrie would let me have any visitors!"

"She didn't let us in," Jay whispered. "We sneaked in. The same way we're going to sneak you out."

"Sneak me out?" Mr. Whitson asked. "What kind of a joke is this?"

"It's no joke," Cindy said urgently. "We're trying to help you escape from here."

"I found Cassie's letters," Jay said. "She was writing to you all the time. I found the letters hidden in the lake. Lorrie and John and even Guy Sanderson have been in on a scheme to rob you and Cassie of this island."

"Cassie didn't write that letter saying she was going to sell to a big resort. *They* did," Cindy added.

Mr. Whitson covered his face with his gnarled old hands and rocked back and forth. "Letters? From Cassie?"

"You've got to believe us," urged Cindy. "There isn't much time. We've got to get out of here."

Mr. Whitson straightened in his chair. "I do believe you, child. I may be old, but I am not an old fool." He glanced around at the room, at the books scattered everywhere.

Jay followed the old man's eyes. "We can always come back later and get your books," he said. "But now we have to hurry. Lorrie and John are down at the pier with Guy. He thinks we're going to hand over the will, but Dexter's downstairs right now exchanging the real will with blank papers. Those three crooks will get exactly what they deserve—nothing."

Mr. Whitson smiled broadly. "I can still enjoy a charade," he said. "Fetch me my cane, son."

The trio walked slowly to the door. "Let me check," Jay said, opening the door a crack and listening. He hoped that Guy hadn't decided to come back right away.

But everything was quiet. Jay nodded to Cindy and the old man. They edged through the door, and Cindy shut it softly behind them. They shuffled down the long hallway to the stairway, Mr. Whitson's grip tight on his cane.

10 • To the Rescue!

THE STAIRWAY WAS steep and long, and Cindy looked worriedly at Mr. Whitson. With her and Jay at each side, and his cane, they'd probably make a lot of noise. And it would take so *long*. How much time did they have left before Guy came for the papers? It seemed as though an hour had passed already. Was Dexter still looking for the will in the basement? He *couldn't* get caught, he just couldn't. Cindy bit her lip and stared again at the steep descent of the stairs.

"We're moving too slowly—I'd like to try something," Mr. Whitson whispered. He gave his cane to Cindy as she and Jay stared at him. "Just give me a hand up," he said, grabbing hold of the bannister.

Cindy's eyes widened. "You're not going to slide down the bannister?" she asked in disbelief.

"I am," Mr. Whitson whispered back firmly. "I used to when I was a kid, and I feel like a kid again for the first time in years. A hand up, please."

Jay and Cindy exchanged glances. Mr. Whitson was frail. But was the bannister strong enough to support him?

"It's our only way," Mr. Whitson said. "Don't worry, the bannister is sturdy enough. It would take me fifteen minutes to walk down these stairs. Now, a hand?"

Jay and Cindy helped him up. He was light and surprisingly agile. "It's just my legs that give me trouble," Mr. Whitson whispered encouragingly.

The two Spotlighters hardly had to hold onto the old man at all. He slid quietly down the bannister as Cindy and Jay hurried alongside, ready to catch him if he lost his balance. In less than a minute they had descended the stairs.

Wordlessly, Jay and Cindy helped Mr. Whitson

down off the bannister and handed him his cane. The old man chuckled softly. He pointed his cane to the front door and nodded. They moved carefully from the bottom of the steps to the door.

In another moment, they were quietly making their way in the dark toward the beach.

While Jay and Cindy were upstairs, Dexter was in the basement, searching for the workroom where the old desk was supposed to be. Everything down here smelled musty and mildewed. He'd turned on the switch at the top of the stairs as Guy had suggested, but there were only two lightbulbs in the entire basement and they were dim.

He'd have to hurry. Dexter started over to the corner of the big basement room where a door stood ajar. It was the only door in sight. It had to lead to the workroom.

Dexter pushed the door open. There was a desk in one corner of the small room.

Guy had said to look in the right-hand side of the desk, the third drawer down. Dexter reached for the handle and pulled. The drawer didn't budge. Locked, he thought with panic. Guy hadn't said anything about a lock. Maybe John or Lorrie had decided to lock it to be extra safe.

But Dexter yanked again, and the drawer creaked open. A musty odor wafted up as he hurriedly felt through the stacks of papers, envelopes, and what felt like newspaper clippings. There it was. A thick brown folder with a cord around it. He slid the cord off and peered inside. The will. Guy wouldn't get it now. He wouldn't get it, ever.

Dexter rummaged in the drawer until he found

a large envelope. He put the will in it and placed the envelope under his shirt next to his skin.

Then he stuffed the manilla folder with other loose papers that were in the drawer.

Closing the drawer quietly, Dexter had a sudden inspiration. He tied strong, tiny knots in the cord around the brown envelope. Cutting the knots wouldn't hold Guy off for very long, but every minute was important.

Dexter stood, listening. He heard the floor creaking above him. Was it Cindy and Jay with Mr. Whitson? Or was Guy back already, suspecting something? Would Guy come back before Cindy and Jay had a chance to get away with Mr. Whitson? He barely breathed, trying to listen. The creaking stopped.

Taking a deep breath, he ran up the basement stairs to the kitchen. As he headed for the front hallway, he heard heavy footsteps on the porch steps.

The doorknob turned, and Dexter stood face to face with Guy. Guy hadn't wasted any time. Had Cindy and Jay got away? Or were they still upstairs? Dexter forced a smile.

"All set?" Guy asked in a hoarse, excited whisper. He looked at the folder Dexter held in his hands.

"Yep," Dexter said casually. The papers inside his shirt felt bulky and obvious.

"That's the envelope, all right," Guy said, reaching for it.

If Guy knew what was really inside, Dexter thought, what would he do? He handed the folder to Guy, his heart pounding.

"Hey," Guy said. "Where's your girl friend, Cindy? Still in the basement?"

"She's near the dock, waiting for the police to come." Dexter knew that the police weren't really coming and that Guy wasn't planning on taking them back to the Beeches'. What *was* he planning? After all, the Spotlighters could tell the police a lot of interesting things.

"You wait there too," Guy said, his eyes on the envelope. "I've got to find some tools in the basement. The police should be here soon."

Dexter turned to the front door casually. "I'll see you in a few minutes," he said. Just let me get out the front door, he added to himself.

"Hey!" Guy spoke sharply. Dexter felt the hair on the back of his neck stand up. Had Guy seen the bulge in Dexter's shirt? Did he guess Dexter had switched the papers?

"Yep?" Dexter asked, not turning around.

"Keep out of sight of Lorrie and John. They're still down at the pier waiting for me. It wouldn't do you any good for them to see you, you know. John has a temper. And a gun."

"Right," Dexter said. He opened the door and closed it carefully behind him.

He looked around to make sure that Guy wasn't watching him through a window. He walked slowly until he was sure he was out of sight of the house, then he ran to the chain-link fence.

Jay was there at the gate, waiting. "It worked, it worked!" he said, trying to keep his voice low. "We got Mr. Whitson out. He and Cindy are down at the rowboat."

"And here is the will," said Dexter, pulling the envelope out of his shirt. "Give it to Mr. Whitson and Cindy. They've got to get off quickly." He hesitated. "Why don't you go with them? I'll catch up in Guy's boat."

"Not on your life," said Jay, clapping Dexter on the back. "We'll go together. I'd go with you now, but Mr. Whitson's got to get away."

"Wait for me on the beach and be ready to wade out to Guy's boat when I bring it around," said Dexter.

Jay hesitated. "Be careful," he warned.

Dexter nodded. "Just get Cindy and Mr. Whitson away from the island."

Jay started toward the beach where Cindy waited with Mr. Whitson and the rowboat. He kept a firm grip on the envelope.

Dexter made his way stealthily through the woods. He could see the lights in the house. What was Guy doing? Had he discovered that Mr. Whitson was gone and the papers had been switched? Dexter swallowed and kept moving as quietly and as quickly as he could.

As he neared the dock, he heard the voices of John and Lorrie. Quickly he plotted his strategy. All he needed was a minute, maybe two, at the boats. Somehow he'd have to get John and Lorrie away from there. Then he'd take the keys from John's boat so they couldn't use it. He'd start Guy's boat. Lucky, after all, they'd had that time with Guy this morning, out fishing. He knew exactly how to run the boat. He'd go around the island, pick up Jay, and they'd be off. There was no way Guy could follow. Dexter smiled.

How could he get Lorrie and John away from the dock? Dexter had an idea. Kneeling on the ground, he felt around for stones, twigs—anything he could throw that could make a splash. He paused for a moment, listening.

"What's taking Guy so long?" Lorrie asked. "It's taking him forever to find a silly old screwdriver."

"Relax—you're just nervous. We're in good shape now. We've got the will, signed and safe. We won't have to give Guy a thing. He'll be back in a minute. We've got to get the boat fixed if we're going to get out of here tomorrow."

Dexter heaved a handful of small stones as hard as he could. He heard them splash. Lorrie uttered a small, shrill cry. "What's that?"

Hurriedly, Dexter gathered another handful and threw them in the same direction.

"I'm not waiting here for Guy another second,"

Lorrie said. "There's an animal of some kind around here, and it's coming closer."

"All right. Let's go up to the house. I'll get my gun," said John. "I hate this place!"

The two left the dock and started through the woods. Dexter waited only a few seconds. Then he made a dash to the pier.

He'd take John's keys and throw them into the water. He felt for the ignition.

No keys.

He went over to Guy's boat, his heart pounding. What if he and Jay couldn't get away after all?

No keys here, either. And no oars.

Dexter crouched, motionless. His heart sank. They were trapped.

Dexter knew he had to do something and do it fast. The hoax would be discovered any minute.

It looked as if he and Jay couldn't get away now. They'd have to hide. But at least Cindy was safe. And Mr. Whitson.

Dexter made a decision. He untied both boats and then pushed them, one at a time, as hard as he could away from the pier. There was enough of a breeze to carry them away—far enough away, he hoped, so that Guy or Lorrie or John couldn't swim after them.

Then Dexter headed through the woods toward the other side of the island. He knew Jay would be on the beach waiting for him—waiting for him to come in Guy's boat. Together they would have to figure out some other way to escape. They'd have to!

Already Dexter felt he knew his way around the small island. His heart beat wildly from running and from fear.

Dexter saw Jay sitting on the beach. "It's me," he whispered as he drew near. "I couldn't get the boat. The keys are missing."

"What can we do?" Jay said.

Suddenly they heard voices, angry voices. "They've found out that Mr. Whitson is gone," said Jay. "They know they've been tricked."

The voices were getting louder. "Here they come." Jay looked around desperately. "We could hide in the reeds."

"Reeds!" said Dexter excitedly. "Into the water," he whispered. "We'll hide under the water and use reeds to breathe. Remember when we did that at camp?"

Jay and Dexter quickly waded into the lake. Jay yanked two reeds from the dark water. He bit off the ends and handed one of the reeds to Dexter. Just in time. Guy's big form came running out of the woods. The boys put the ends of their reeds in their mouths and ducked under water. Only their reeds showed above the surface. They breathed through their mouths.

Jay could feel Dexter close beside him. The lake was shallow here, and it was hard to stay underwater. He tugged at Dexter's arm and headed out into deeper water, holding onto roots to keep himself from floating to the surface. Jay wished they could hear what Lorrie, John, and Guy were saying.

Jay breathed steadily through his reed, but he couldn't suck in any more air. Somehow dirt must have lodged in the hollow of the reed. Keep calm, he told himself, fighting the urge to push his head above water. He blew harder, trying to dislodge the obstruction, but he couldn't. Seconds passed. He had to come up for air.

He put his face up above the water and breathed deeply. He realized the voices had stopped. Only the sound of the frogs reached his ears. Had Guy and

Lorrie and John gone? Or were they hiding? Would they be back—with a flashlight?

Dexter was still underwater. Jay swam the couple of feet over to him and tapped his shoulder. "They've gone," he whispered when Dexter surfaced. "Maybe they're looking for us at the pier. Maybe they're getting the boats."

"They won't find them," Dexter said confidently.

"They'll find us, though," said Jay. "We can't hide underwater all night. We've got to figure out a way to escape from the island. If only we had another boat!"

Suddenly he snapped his fingers. "That canoe—the birchbark canoe Mr. Whitson said he'd worked on. It's at the side of the house. Remember?"

Dexter grinned in the dark and slapped Jay on the back. Dripping wet, they moved carefully out of the water and onto the tiny beach. In a moment they were slipping through the woods on their way to the birchbark canoe.

They could hear voices, Guy's and John's. Then an angry scream, Lorrie's scream. The three of them had discovered that the boats were gone.

There was no time to lose. Maybe Guy could

swim out and get his boat. Maybe—and maybe he'd catch up with Cindy and Mr. Whitson.

The boys moved quickly. The canoe was where they'd seen it before. And under the canoe, a paddle. "Thank heaven!" Dexter whispered.

The boys hoisted the canoe onto their shoulders and headed back toward the beach. Dexter glanced behind him. He could see a light bobbing in the trees.

"Hurry," Dexter whispered to Jay. At last the boys reached the beach. They put the canoe right side up in the water. Now they could hear footsteps and voices, coming close. Suddenly the flashlight played along the water. Dexter and Jay pulled the canoe behind a clump of weeds. If they tried to climb in and paddle away now, they'd be seen.

"Let's turn the boat upside down and paddle toward the channel," whispered Dexter. "We can breathe under it in the air pocket. The canoe will be low on the water and they might not spot it."

Guy bellowed, "How did they do it? The other one, the blond kid, is locked in the boathouse. How did the other two foul me up?"

"You must have done something stupid," whined Lorrie. "Why on earth are we even looking for those two kids here? They're not here, anyone can plainly see that. And they haven't got a way off the island any more than we have. They must be hiding in the woods somewhere."

Jay kicked Dexter gently under the water and the boys started to inch the canoe slowly away from the island. Lifting up his end of the boat a little, Dexter could make out the opening of the channel. They kicked slowly, purposefully, under the water. They had at least a hundred yards to go.

Paddling under the canoe, slowly, they made their way to the channel. The angry, bewildered voices still came clearly across the water.

Suddenly a spotlight shone on them. They'd been seen!

"There they are!" shouted Guy, his voice hoarse with excitement and anger. In another moment Dexter and Jay had turned into the channel, out of sight.

"Get them! You've got to get them!" demanded Lorrie in a shrill scream.

Dexter and Jay righted the boat and tried to climb in. "I forget how we do this," whispered Dexter urgently.

"Me too," groaned Jay. "It seemed easy at camp."

"We rock the canoe back and forth," said Dexter.

"I'll get them," shouted Guy, his voice knifing through the dark night. "I'm the strongest swimmer in these parts."

There was a loud splash.

"Guy's coming after us," whispered Jay. "Hurry."

With sudden strength Dexter swung himself into the canoe, and in a moment Jay joined him.

Dexter dipped the paddle strongly into the water.

"I'll get you!" came Guy's shout.

There was more splashing and then another, different shout. One of pain. "My ankle! That big rock!"

"Swim anyway!" cried Lorrie.

The boys maneuvered the canoe through the twisting channel.

Suddenly they stiffened. What was that shape, looming ahead? Was it John? Had he somehow managed to get away to head them off?

Then a voice called softly through the night. "Jay? Dex?"

It was Cindy. "Mr. Whitson wouldn't let me leave," she explained. "Not until you were safe."

"We've made it!" Mr. Whitson cried, his voice strong and happy. "You three with your guts and soft hearts and me with…with…"

"With Cassie and your island," Cindy finished for him.

"And us as your friends!" Dexter and Jay said from the canoe.

The three Spotlighters and Mr. Whitson laughed. Everything was all right now. Soon they'd be in Mr. Beech's cabin with the police.

"Cassie, here I come!" Mr. Whitson shouted.

The small rowboat moved steadily on, with the canoe right behind it.

About the authors Florence Parry Heide and Roxanne Heide have no trouble thinking of exciting adventures for the Spotlight Club detectives. Often this mother-daughter team meet at a family lakeside cottage in Wisconsin, spend several days with their typewriters, and emerge with the plot for a story. More conferences, phone calls, letters, and perhaps another meeting, and a new mystery is ready.

Florence Heide brings versatility and enthusiasm to all she does. She's written lyrics for songs, picture books (including the popular THE SHRINKING OF TREEHORN), short novels for teen readers, and stories for reading programs, as well as the Spotlight Club mystery series. Roxanne Heide has produced textbook material and collaborated on many mysteries in the Spotlight Club series, as well as on the Brillstone mysteries, another series published by Albert Whitman.

About the illustrator Seymour Fleishman is a Chicago artist who has worked in book illustration, advertising, and design. He has illustrated many books for children, including the Spotlight Club series. Mr. Fleishman has also written and illustrated PRINTCRAFTS, a book that presents ways children can print their own stationery, announcements, and newspapers.